MERMAID'S COVE

By Jeanette Mc Farlane

For Gabrielle

The sweetest little girl who showed compassion for others at such a young age.

Once upon a time in the sparkling waters of the ocean, there was a place called Mermaid's Cove. Many Mer-families lived there. They were happy there. They were careful not to be seen by humans. There were four teenage mermaids with special talents. Jellica, Star, Findella and Sandy.

Jellica had the talent of shocking and stinging with her hands. She had pink hair, blue eyes and a blue tail. Jellica loves the color pink and she loves to find pink shells. She has a collection of pink treasures. She really likes finding human objects. She loves finding special things for her friends. She was a very giving mermaid.

Star had the talent of seeing and hearing things far away. She also had a beautiful singing voice. Star had blonde hair, green eyes and a green tail. Star was very concerned about her appearance. She did not like her hair out of place. Star uses starfish and human objects to keep her hair in place.

Findella had a super strong tail. She could swim fast and move things with her tail. Findella was brave and athletic. She had blue hair, light purple eyes and a blue tail. She had no fear of humans, even though mermaids were forbidden contact with humans, because most humans did not believe in mermaids.

Sandy could make strong currents with her tail and push away most of the dangerous sea creatures. Sandy had black hair, brown eyes and a green tail. Sandy had a little brother ,named Kelpen and a little sister, named Angel. Sandy helped her mom with her brother and sister and she enjoyed them.

There were also three teenage mer-girls, who called themselves the Hardshells. They did not like the talented mer-girls. They were jealous of them.

There was Shellyn, who was very pretty. She was stuck-up and selfish. She thought she was the most beautiful mermaid. She had blonde hair, aqua eyes and a aqua tail.

Scarlett had red hair, amber eyes and a orange tail. She was also selfish and did not like to share. She liked to be the leader of the group.

And Krabell.

Krabell was kind of a grump and liked to make jokes about other mermaids. She had brown hair, green eyes and a blue tail.

One day when Angel, Kelpen

and the mer-kids were getting out of mer-school,

they decided to play swim and seek. They

started swimming right by the school, hiding

behind rocks, plants and their favorite spot a

sunken pirate ship. The mer-kids were having so

much fun they didn't realize they had swam

away from mermaids cove and into Shark

Territory. Angel found a small cave to hide in.

She was waiting for her friends to find her when

she saw a big tiger shark swim by the cave.

Angel shook with fear, sharks scare her very

much. Angel swam back in the cave as far as she

could. Kelpen swam up to the cave. "I see you

Angel!" Cried Kelpen. "Kelpen, get in the cave

quick, there is a shark!" Said Angel. Kelpen swam into the cave and held Angel. "Don't worry Angel, we'll be okay." Angel thought for a moment then said, "We have to call Star, She will hear us and bring help." "Star, come help us, there is a shark!" They cried. The other mer-kids had already swam home.

Back in her coral reef room Star was singing and brushing her long hair when she heard Angel and Kelpens cry for help. When she heard them she dropped the human brush Jellica had found for her and swam off to find the mer-girls. Star found Findella and Jellica on there way to

Sandy's home. "Girls, Angel and Kelpen are in trouble, They are in a cave, with a shark outside!" Star exclaimed. "Lets go get Sandy." Said Jellica. The mer-girls found Sandy at home helping her mom make seaweed lasagna. "Sandy, Angel and Kelpen are in trouble, they need our help." Cried Star. "Oh my goodness!" Sandy's mom said, "Hurry girls!" "I will get us there fast. Everyone hold hands." Said Findella. Findella used her super speed and took them to Angel and Kelpen. The mergirls hid behind a large rock. They saw the shark circling the cave waiting for them to come out. "Jellica try shocking the shark." Sandy said. Jellica put up her hands and started shocking the shark. The shark jerked, but kept circling the cave. "It's not working. Help me Sandy, use your currents." Jellica said. Sandy used her tail and a strong current was created. After a while the shark got tired of being shocked and swimming against the current and swam away. Angel and Kelpen swam out of the cave. Sandy hugged her brother and sister. "Are you okay?' Asked Sandy. "Yes." Replied Angel. "Let's go home you two, mom is very worried." "Everyone hold on I'll take us back." Said Findella. Everyone held

hands and Findella took them to Sandy's home.
Sandy's mom was very relieved. "If you two
scare me like that again, your in big trouble!"
She said, then she thanked the mer-girls.
"Thank-you for saving my babies." "Well that
was fun." Jellica said. "It sure messed up my
hair." Said Star. "Don't worry Star, I found
some pink shells you can use for your hair."
said Jellica. "Oh I can't wait to see them!" Cried
Star. The mer-girls had to go home so they said
goodbye to each other.

There was to be a
Mermaid's Ball. The mer-girls were very excited

about it. They were in Star's room talking about it. "Jellica, you must find the most exquisite shells and barrettes." Said Star, "I will help you all with your hair." "I wonder if Ray is going, he's so cute!" Said Sandy. Ray was the mer-boy Sandy liked. "Isn't Ray going with Shellyn?" Asked Findella. "No, they broke-up." Said Jellica. "It's looking good for you, Sandy." Said Star. "Lets go to the shore and see what we can find." Said Jellica. And off they swam in search of things for the Mer-ball.

Jellica's father was in charge of making the ballroom. The mer-girls were all helping decorate. They used glittering starfish, shells, seaweed and human objects Jellica found. It turned out very nice.

Findella and Sandy were swimming near the shore, looking for things for the ball.

They surfaced their heads and looked to see if

any humans were about. It was a beautiful day

the sun was shinning bright. The coast was clear,

so to shore they went. Something shinny caught

Jellica's eyes. "Look at this!" Jellica cried. It was a beautiful pearl and diamond bracelet and matching barrette. "Oh it's so pretty, you know Star will flip over these." Findella said. Sifting through the sand they found some hair pins, rubber bands, a few toys and a parasol. On their swim back home, they swam into Ray and his friend Finnous. "Hey girls." Said Ray. "Hi" Replied Sandy. "Hey Sandy, will you go to the ball with me?" Asked Ray. Sandy smiled big and said, "Oh I would love to!" Finnous swam up to Findella and asked, "Would you go with me?" Findella was surprised but glad. "Yes I will." She said. "That's great!, catch you girls later." Ray said as they swam away. Sandy let out an excited scream. "Can you believe it! It's pearlatious, it's shellious, it's fintastic!" "I know, and Fineous asked me! Let's go tell Jellica and Star."

Meanwhile the Hard shells were in Scarlett's room, talking about the ball. "Can you believe Ray asked Sandy to the ball." Said Scarlett. Shellyn frowned and cried, "How could he not take me? I am the most beautiful mermaid in the sea!" "So you keep telling us." Replied

Krabell. "Well it's true, I should be Ray's date." muttered Shellyn. "Looks like he's over you, guess your Ray of sunshine will be shinning on Sandy." Laughed Krabell. "Clam up Krabell.' Said Shellyn. "Listen, I have a plan to get even with those soft shells." Said Scarlett. "Let's steal all the things they are planning on wearing to the ball". They all agreed. "Yeah we'll show them." Shellyn said. The night before the ball they would steal their treasures.

Star was with Findella watching Findella doing her back flips for her mer-ball dance, when she heard a call for help. "Findella someone is in trouble," said Star. "Can you see where?" Asked Findella. Star looked in the direction she heard the voice. "Not yet, but it's coming from that way." Star pointed. Star grabbed Findella's hand and they swam to the sound. Not to far from the shore, there was a rock slide. A mermaid was caught by a big boulder. The bottom of her tail was caught. "Oh please help me." She cried.

"Findella use your tail to move the boulder."

Said Star. Findella went to work and used her

powerful tail to push the boulder. In a few

minutes Findella moved the boulder off the

mermaid. "Oh, thank-you", said the mermaid. "I

thought no one would hear me. I was starting to worry. You must come to my house for some sea candy." "Are you alright?" Asked Findella. "Yes", said the mermaid. The girls took her home and had some sea candy, then took some back for their friends.

It was the day before the ball. The mer-girls were getting everything ready. The ballroom looked beautiful. The sparkling shells, decorations and seaweed on the coral reef turned out nicely. "I want to like nice for Ray", said Sandy. "You will, the diamond bracelet and barrette will look lovely", said Star. "I hope so,

Ray is so cute!" Sandy said. "Finnous is cute too!" Added Findella. "What fun I can't wait." said Jellica.

Back at the hard-shell hang out, Shellyn said, "I got Octavy to take me to the ball." "How did you get him to ask you, he's very popular." Said Scarlett. "Who can resist beautiful me?' Asked Shellyn. "Ray can." Krabell answered. "Put a shell in it Krabell." Shellyn fired back. "Me and Octavy will be mer-king and mer-queen." "'Well me and Dareon will win the dance contest." Scarlett said. "I wish I could see those soft shells faces when they see their stuff has disappeared." Said Krabell. "It's almost midnight." Scarlett said. "Let's get ready."

The blue ocean was dark, but still lit by the full moon. The hard shells swam quietly to each mer-girls home and took all the treasure they could find. They were very quiet and did not wake the mer-girls. When they got to Jellica's and Scarlett saw the diamond barrette and bracalet she snached them up. When they got back to their hang out, they laughed. "that was great!", said Krabell. "This pearl and diamond bracelet and barrette are mine", declared

Scarlett. "I don't think so Scarlett, I am the most beautiful mermaid.", said Shellyn. "Don't you ever get tired of saying that, because I sure get tired of hearing it." Krabell moaned. "I wish I could be there to see their faces when they wake up." Scarlett said. "They think they are all that. When I am the most beautiful." Stated Shellyn as she smoothed her hair. "There she goes again, she sounds like a broken shell." Muttered Krabell. The hard shells divided up the rest of the treasure and went to their own homes.

The next morning Sandy stretched her arms and tail and got up. She looked around her room and saw her treasures were gone! She was stunned. She quickly looked under her sponge bed to see if the current had swept them under there. Nothing. She looked all around her room. They were gone. Sandy swam to Star's home. "Star, my things for the ball are gone!" Cried Sandy. "I know, my things are gone too." Star said sadly. Findella and Jellica arrived. "Our things are gone too." They said. "I'll bet I know who did this, the Hardshells I would like to give them a sting." Said Jellica. "You know that's forbidden, but I would like to give them a whack with my tail." Said Findella.

"What are we going to do?' Cried Sandy. "How will I look nice for Ray now?" "Don't worry, I'll fix everyone's hair and we still have time to find shells and starfish." Said Star. "If Ray doesn't think you are beautiful already, who needs him." Said Findella. "She's right Sandy, we will still have a great time." Jellica said.

The following day Findella and Sandy were swimming near the surface, heading to the shore. Above them in a fishing boat, was a 12 year old girl named Gabrielle.

Gabrielle was with her father. Gabrielle was a

very pretty child with golden blonde hair and

sky blue eyes. She was a very caring girl too.

Gabrielle was watching her father bring in fish

with a fishing net. Something glittered in the

water and caught Gabrielle's eye. What could

that be thought Gabrielle. Something she had never seen before. Findella was close to the surface when the net was dropped. Findella was caught!

Findella saw the net on her tail and started to panic. "Sandy!" Screamed Findella. "Findella, clam down, it's okay, use your tail to get out of the net." Sandy said. Findella calmed down and used her tail to get out of the net. Gabrielle watched wide-eyed, not sure of what she was seeing. Could that really be a mermaid? She loved them, but didn't think they existed. She thought Findella was beautiful. She couldn't wait to go to shore and look for her. "Are you okay Findella?" Asked Sandy. "My fin is twisted and it hurts. How will I do the dance contest now?" Replied Findella. "I'm sorry."

Star said, as she put her arm around her. "I'll help you swim home."

While Findella and Sandy were out looking for more treasure, so was Jellica. Jellica swam through an old pirate ship looking for something they might have missed. She noticed the ship had holes in it. She wondered how the humans lived on it and what had made the big hole on the side that must have made it sink. She didn't find anything, so she swam on. Jellica swam through caves and explored the ocean floor. She was about to give up when she saw something sparkle. She quickly swam to it.

Jellica stopped. Glittering on the bottom was a wishing starfish!

What luck! Jellica did a happy little swim and scooped up the starfish. Wishing starfish were very rare. They gave mermaids one wish.

Excited, Jellica hurried and swam back to show her friends.

Star was just outside her home when Jellica swam up. "Star you will never believe what I found! A wishing starfish!" Cried Jellica. "Wow ! That's fintastic! Where did you find it?" Asked Star." I found it on the ocean floor, by the pretty sea garden we found.' "Now we can wish for treasure for the ball!" Star said. Just then Findella and Sandy swam up. "I have bad news girls, Findella was caught in a net and she twisted her fin." Said Sandy. "Now I can't be in the dance contest." Findella said sadly. Jellica saw the look on Findella's face and said instantly, "Findella, I found a wishing star today, please use it and heal your fin." "Oh Jellica I can't take that from you they are so rare." Replied Findella. "I really want you to have it. You are more important to me than any hair piece or jewelry. And I love watching you dance." Jellica said. "Okay, thank-you so much Jellica." Said Findella and gave Jellica a hug. "Make your wish Findella." Said Jellica as she handed her the glittering wishing starfish with a big smile on face. It meant a lot to her to help her friend. Findella took the wishing starfish and said, "I wish my fin was healed." Sparkles swirled around her tail and fins. Then Findella's fin was healed!"You will show those Hardshells who wins the dance contest." Said Star. "I can't thank-you enough Jellica." Said Findella.

Later that day Gabrielle went down to the shore.

She waited there to see if the mermaids would

show up. After an hour and a half Jellica and

Findella swam close to shore. They had their

heads out of the water and the back of their fins

were showing. They did not see Gabrielle.

Gabrielle stared wide eyed again. She still could not believe it. She pinched herself to make sure she was awake. She was. Gabrielle just stared at them for several moments. It was the most beautiful sight she had ever seen. She could not believe their beauty. They had very delicate features. Their hair was long, strange colors, but shinny, their tails glittered. Gabrielle held her breath trying to get the courage to walk over to them. She wanted to talk to them. She wanted to be their friend. Hopefully they would understand English. Gabrielle took a deep breath and stepped forward. "Hello." She said. Jellica and

Findella looked up with shock on their faces and started to swim away. "Please don't go! I won't hurt you!" Cried Gabrielle. Jellica and Findella paused, not sure they could trust her. They had never talked to a human before. "Please don't leave. I saw you caught in my father's fishing net. He didn't see you and I didn't tell him. I love mermaids! I'm so happy your real I won't tell anyone." "Findella we should go." Jellica said. "No I have a good feeling about her. I think we can trust her." Said Findella. "My name is Gabrielle. I want to be your friend." "My name is Findella and this is Jellica." Said Findella.

"Wow those are really cool names." Said Gabrielle. "How many mermaids are there?" "There is about 40-50 of us I would guess. In this part of the ocean." said Jellica. "That's wonderful! What are you doing here?" Asked Gabrielle. She couldn't believe she was talking to mermaids! "We are having a mermaids ball and we were looking for things to put in our hair." Answered Jellica. Gabrielle pulled the barrettes from her hair and said, "Here take these and I can bring you more tomorrow." "You don't have to do that." Said Findella. "Oh I want to, I have so many. I want to be your friend. I think you are beautiful. What do you do all day?" Asked Gabrielle. "Well we help with the mer-kids, we go to school, we look for human objects, we help other mermaids." said Findella. "What's a mermaid ball?" asked Gabrielle. "Well it's a night of dancing and there will be a mer-queen and king." Said Jellica. "Can you keep seeing us a secert?" "Oh yes I won't tell anyone." Said Gabrielle. "How would you like to meet two of our friends?" Asked Findella. "Yes yes yes!" said Gabrielle jumping up and down. "Okay we will send Star and Sandy tomorrow to met you. It was nice meeting you.

Now remember, don't tell anyone." Jellica reminded her. "Oh I won't cross my heart. I am so happy I met you! I can't wait to meet your friends!" "Bye for now Gabrielle." The mer-girls said. Findella and Jellica made a splash with their tails and swam off. Gabrielle watched them swim away. Then she jumped up and down. "I met mermaids! I met mermaids! This is a dream come true!" She was so happy. Then she ran home.

Findella and Jellica swam back to their homes. "That was close." Jellica said. "Yes, but she was nice I trust her." Replied Findella. They told Star and Sandy about her but no one else. When Star and Sandy found out Star said "A human girl! Have you lost your scales? Are you sure you can trust her?" "Yes , I have a good feeling about her." said Findella. "What's she like?" Asked Sandy. " She's very cute and sweet. She saw Findella caught in her father's fishing net and she didn't tell him." Said Jellica. "And look she gave us these." Said Findella., Holding out her hand with the barrettes. "You can met her if you like, she will be back on the shore tomorrow." "Oh We would love to met her! A human girl!" Said Star and Sandy. They all agreed this would be their secert.

The next day Sandy and Star went to shore to met Gabrielle. Gabrielle was there, excited as ever. "Oh my, on my, I still can't believe this!" she exclaimed. She watched as Sandy and Star gracefully swam towards the shore. They were so beautiful! "Hello!" Called Gabrielle, "I'm Gabrielle, your so pretty, I'm so happy to meet you!" "I'm Star and this is Sandy." Said Star, pointing to Sandy. "I brought you these hair ties and pins." Said Gabrielle. "Thank-you, and your pretty too." Said Sandy. Star heard humans talking far away on their way down to the shore. "Someone's coming, we have to go. It was nice meeting you, Gabrielle." Star said. "Oh, I am so happy I met you! This is a dream come true! I will come back whenever you like." Said Gabrielle. "It's a deal. We are glad we met you too. You're the first Human we have ever talked to." Said Sandy. "Bye for now." "Bye." Said Gabrielle. Sandy and Star dove into the sea, their tails splashing on the surface. Gabrielle watched them swim away. Then she did a little dance and jumped up and down. She was so happy! What a wonderful Day!

It was finally the day of the

Mermaids Ball. Star had all the mer-girls in her

room. "Is everyone excited?" Said Star. "I will

fix everyone's hair now."

For Findella she put her hair half up and half down with a starfish. For Jellica she gave her two ponytails and wrapped them up. For Sandy she put her hair up with braids around it. Then added the pink barrettes Gabrielle gave her. And for herself she put her hair up and placed shells around it. "You all look beautiful, I do good work." Star said. They all thanked her. "Okay it's time to go, but let's swim slow. We don't want to mess up our hair." Said Star. And off they went.

Back at the Hardshells hang out, They were getting ready too. "Let's show those soft shells who is going to be the winner's tonight." Said Scarlett. "I know I will be Mer Queen ." Said Shellyn. "Oh Please, not again." Moaned Krabell. "Time to go, let's swim." Said Scarlett. The Hardshells left for the Mer- Ball.

The mer-grls arrived at the ball. Fineous and Ray swam over. "You look so pretty Sandy." "Thank-you." said Sandy to Ray. "You look pretty too Findella." Said Fineous. "Thanks, You look nice too. " Said Findella. The mer-girls all smiled at each other. "Would you like to dance Sandy?" Asked Ray. "Yes, I would." Sandy answered. Findella and Fineous joined them.

The Hardsheels were watching the couples dance. Shellyn was so jealous of Sandy. "I can't wait to laugh in Sandy's face when Octavy win Mer-king and Queen." She said. "You better hope you're the one laughing." Krabell told her.

The mer-girls were having a wonderful time. Star and Jellica got asked to dance too. Then it was time for the dance contest.

"Everyone who wants to be in the dance contest swim over." Said the announcer. Findella and Fineous swam over. So did Scarlett and Dareon. "Hey Findella, Dareon and I have this in the net." Scarlett claimed. "That's what you think. Findella replied. The contest started. Findella and Fineous made it to the finals. So did Scarlett and Dareon. Scarlett gave Findella a confident look. Findella just smiled at her. Not letting Scarlett bother her. The mer-girls cheered on Findella. "Come on Findella you can do it!" They cried. "You better not let those soft shells beat you Scarlett." Cried the Hardshells. Then

Findella really did her thing. She glided gracefully and danced in perfect sync with Fineous. She did her triple back flip, front flip and fast tail work. The crowd cheered. The announcer was ready to name the winner." Second place goes to Scarlett and Dareon." He said. "First place goes to Findella and Fineous." The mer-girls cheered. The first place prize were beautiful sea shell necklaces. "You did really good Scarlett." Said Findella. "Your just a lucky starfish." Scarlett said. The mer-girls hugged Findella. "We are so proud of you!" They said. Scarlett said "Thanks for nothing." to

Dareon, then swam back to the hardshells. "Nice going, what happened? Did you twist your fin?" Cracked Krabell. "I'll break your fin, if you don't clam-up." Replied Scarlett. "Girls There is still the King and Queen contest." Said Shellyn. "Better cross your fins." Said Krabell. "Wait and see, I don't have to cross anything." Claimed Shellyn.

The Ball went on, then it was time to announce the Mer-King and Mer-Queen. "Mermen and mermaids I have the winner's for the King and Queen." Said the announcer. The mer-girls held hands. The Hardshells just

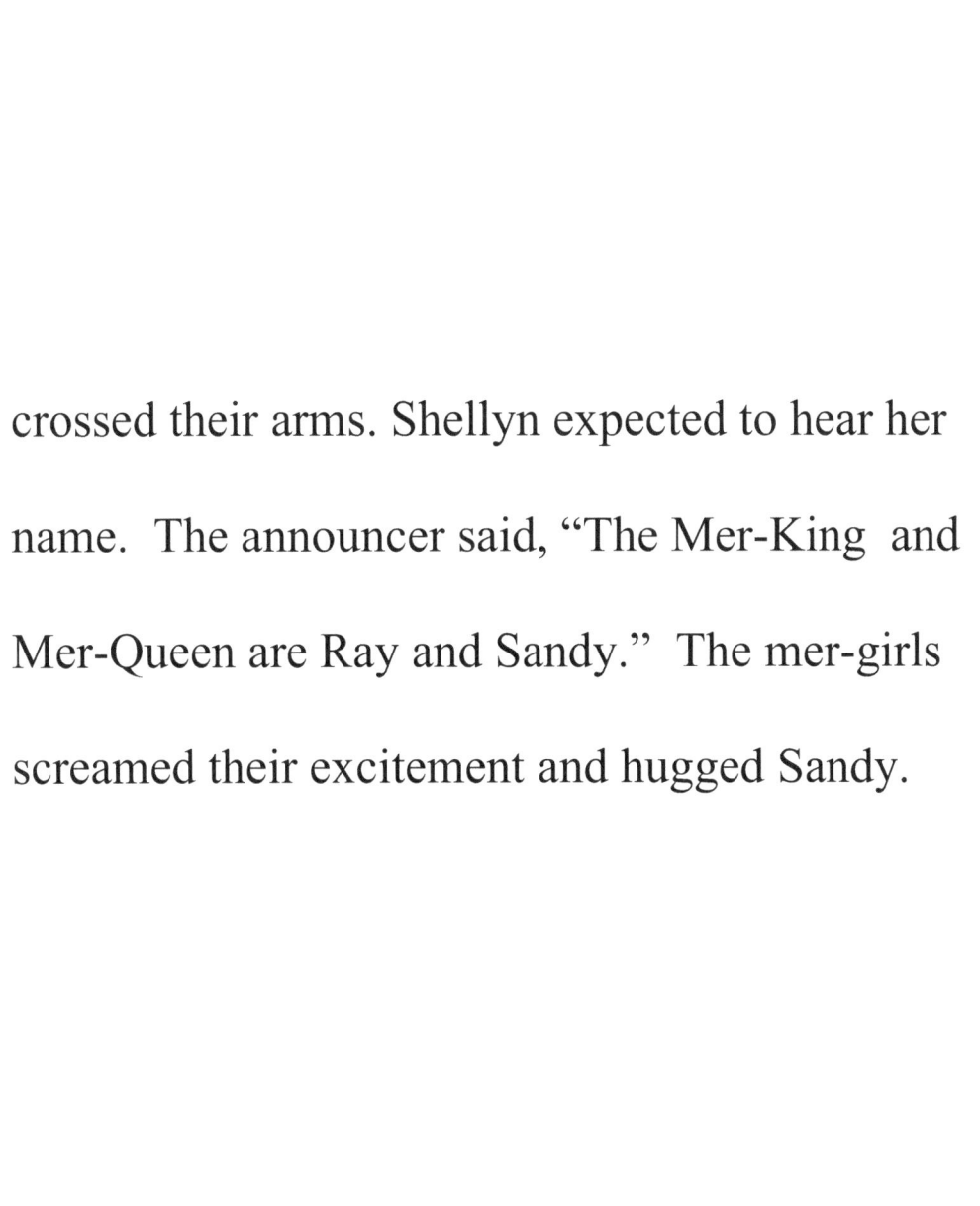

crossed their arms. Shellyn expected to hear her name. The announcer said, "The Mer-King and Mer-Queen are Ray and Sandy." The mer-girls screamed their excitement and hugged Sandy.

The Hardshells glared at them and Krabell said "Ha-ha in your fishface Shellyn." Scarlett who knew how it felt to lose, softened a bit and said," That's enough Krabell, she's still prettier." Shellyn felt better then.

A beautiful crown made of shells and pearls was placed on Sandy's head. A crown of shells and starfish was placed on Ray. "I can't believe it, I can't believe we won!" Cried Sandy. "I can, you are the prettiest mermaid in the ocean." Said Ray. Sandy blushed. Then he kissed her. What a wonderful night! Thought Sandy. The Ball ended, the mer-girls hugged each other. Ray and Fineous swam the mer-girls home. They took Star and Jellica home first, then Fineous swam Findella home and Ray swam Sandy home. When Fineous got to Findella's home he said, "I had a great time.' "Me too. And we won!" said Findella. "I'm not surprised, you're a fantastic dancer." said Fineous. Then Fineous kissed her goodnight. Findella thanked him for taking her and said goodnight. She was very happy. Ray took Sandy home and kissed her goodnight. Sandy thought of the fun night she had and what wonderful friends she had. She knew they would always be friends. The Mer-girls did not even miss the treasure the Hardshells took. Friendship was better than any treasure or human object. And now they had a new human friend, Gabrielle. Sandy knew they would all have sweet dreams this night, look forward to the days ahead and getting to know Gabrielle.

www.ingramcontent.com/pod-product-compliance
Lightning Source LLC
Chambersburg PA
CBHW041026170626
46815CB00001B/16